TITLE

OVER THE MOUNT

By Sidra Mohsin

Grandma's House

It is best 100% of the time to think about existence while taking other factors into consideration. In addition, a cut of lemon (perhaps a lime) and an injection of tequila. Nonetheless, it's the end of the world. Salt would become cash, as would lemons-however just in hotter conditions. Tequila, then again, would be in the bladder of some dead person.

In the present circumstance, tragically, Evelyn couldn't take existence with any of those fixings. The remainder of the salt was utilized above and beyond a year prior in some virus soup. She hadn't seen a lemon since before the end times. The tequila, not-really amusingly, was utilized to sanitize a head wound. However, it wasn't really tequila. It was a half-filled jug of some modest white wine.

"...isn't excessively right?"

Evelyn stumbled over the temporary obstacle, getting herself very quickly. A tree root had gotten through the surface some time back.

"Please accept my apologies, what?" sooner or later Evelyn had become out to lunch. It was no doubt around a similar time she had elapsed what was likely the millionth tree. She, and the gathering with her, had been strolling this way since sun up. Not one thing changed with regards to it aside from an intermittent bend in the asphalt. Trees flanked the disintegrating street on the two sides. For as should have been obvious, there was no carport to be seen.

"In your mind once more?"

Evelyn couldn't prevent herself from separating. With another person driving the gathering rather than her, it was simpler to follow without thinking, particularly since the strolling time frame was moving toward the seventh hour.

"Please accept my apologies, Danny." She delivered a depleted breath. Last time she separated he spoke harshly to her, however they likewise ran into various setbacks that day. "I don't intend to."

"Try not to apologize. I realize you're drained. All of us are drained. Hungry. Parched." He set his arm delicately over her shoulders, cautious to not place more weight on them. "We'll stop when it gets dim."

Evelyn thought it very unusual Daniel rested his arm around her edge. He has never accomplished something to that effect. She chose to put it on exhaustion.

Daniel could detect her adjustment of conduct. "You're shuddering." The main legitimate clarification concerning for what reason he'd show her actual friendship.

Her left arm reluctantly folded over his lower back, holding onto the coarse material of his colder time of year coat. Basically the murkiness assisted with smothering her anxiety. Her ribs turned into even more warm with his extra body heat. Very quickly her muscles loose. The strain disseminated. She wants to talk about these thoughts with her kin. Particularly the children. They need it the most.

One of the kids, Lily May, pulled on Evelyn's free hand, pulling the lady from her daze. Evelyn and Daniel fell to pieces.

"Hello, Lily. What's going on?"

The kid pulled Evelyn down to her level, murmuring something in her ear. Evelyn gestured. She went to Daniel. "I figure we should stop for a restroom break."

Daniel stopped the gathering. Everybody alternated utilizing the woods. Evelyn went last. She strolled behind a tree sufficiently huge enough to cover her body. Barely anything came out. The work it took to arrange her jeans back the manner in which they were was adequately signal enough. Rest calls, as does food and water.

Once back out and about, Evelyn did a head count. Twenty. Ten kids and ten grown-ups, including herself. She got back together with Daniel at the front of the gathering and gestured. Everybody is here and represented.

"Do you actually have that guide on you?" Daniel took out his from his back pocket. Water harm. The tones mixed together in certain areas. It resembled a Monet. A crunchy, firm Monet.

Evelyn held up hers. Same condition. "We have stomach intuition to go off at this point."

"Well crap."

Everybody had strolled for one more hour. Evening time drew closer quicker than they expected. Winter is coming. Trees actually flanked either side of them immediately. Would there be an end? In spite of the little break they had some time prior, nobody felt any better. This appropriate unending reiteration started to destroy their purpose.

Occasionally, Evelyn would pivot to keep an eye on the children. They seemed, by all accounts, to be dialing back. It wouldn't benefit anyone to keep strolling, particularly with no food or water left. They happened upon a crossroads. Two signs stood erect corresponding to the new street. One had a picture of a farm truck. The second, a pony.

Evelyn told Daniel the time had come to stop. As quiet as could be expected, everyone shifted aside from the street. The grown-ups clustered around the kids to keep them warm. They just had whatever they might be wearing, that's it. Some decided to incline facing tree trunks. Others favored the leaf-shrouded floor. No one could be excessively meticulous.

Evelyn couldn't settle in spite of the perpetual measure of events she needed to rest on the woods floor. It was the new standard, yet something jabbed at the rear of her mind. The depletion that saturated her bones asked for rest, yet her brain felt occupied with something different. She stripped her head free and clear, glaring down the two street signs that made her stay totally alert. A sensation of commonality vacillated in her stomach as she kept on concentrating on the signs. It may very well be the appetite torments, but her stomach wouldn't let her credit it to that.

Her eyes moved to the vegetation encompassing the signage. A genuinely huge tree with half of its appendages missing remained behind them. The evening glow enlightened its spooky height, however the actual height showed up practically inviting. Like arms outstretched for a warm embrace. Evelyn needed to go there. Before she even knew what she was going, her legs were taking her to the tree. The hand on her wrist halted her.

"Where are you going?" Daniel moved to get up with her.

"Something doesn't add up about this place..."

They got out of the backwoods, strolling towards the crossroads. Evelyn held up a couple of speeds prior to saying anything to be too far to hear.

"You realize you didn't need to accompany me. It's a couple of yards out." She didn't check out him, just the street ahead.

"Two individuals is more secure than one."

She left it at that, yet had an inclination it was a direct result of that one time she went on all alone and stepped in a bear trap. The scars on her lower leg actually look stained. Daniel recalled that day. Dread desensitized his veins seeing her in such a lot of agony. However, he could never confess to anything.

Evelyn couldn't place her finger on it, however her stomach was advising her to confide in its nature. She approached the sign, shifting her head as she concentrated on it some more. The greater part of the shading was covered by soil and grime, however she could see the pony in any case. Her fingers swiped at the soil on the sign. The first tone appeared differently in relation to the dimness of the evening.

Go left.

She went to one side past Daniel who took a gander at her curiously. He followed not far behind as they strolled this street. Why she decided to go above and beyond could never know. Her body followed some undetectable way in a daze like state while remaining totally mindful. Her eyes floated down to the street. Roots and potholes enlivened it like a Christmas tree, yet Evelyn some way or another kept away from them all. It didn't happen quickly, however the possibility that Evelyn subliminally knew where she was could be the main clarification. Daniel couldn't imagine one more justification for why she would be over here after this street.

All of a sudden, Evelyn ended her means. Daniel ran into her, understanding generally very late he quit focusing. His hands took hold of her hips before she could tumble to the ground.

"Sorry. You alright?" Daniel eliminated his hands once she discovered her balance.

Evelyn gestured, more centered around pulling a memory from the profundities of her brain than the phantom of his hands on her hips. Her sight canvased the way to the timberline. It was stuck barely out of reach of her mind, whatever this feeling was. It was just when the breeze blew somewhat, scattering the light of the moon when it arrived on the splendidly hued letter box not too far off.

Glimmers of her granddad's benevolent eyes went before her. Brief looks at her grandma making dolls without any preparation to put in her stopgap cardboard dollhouse skipped around her vision like a grovel in the snow.

She recalled why that tree with half of its appendages missing caused her to have a solid sense of security and blissful, why it caused her to feel like she would be embraced. This is on the grounds that she would've been. It was the milestone just before the go to her grandparents. An embrace from them was the primary thing she generally got when she went to see them.

"I'm home." She held her hands over her mouth, dropping down to her knees in alleviation. Tears spilled down her cheeks, feeling hot on her chilled skin. Is this a fantasy? She looked into once again, flickering her eyes violently. The post box isn't some delusion. It's there as obvious.

Daniel helped Evelyn dependent upon her feet. She cleaned her tears with her sleeve. "We really want to go get the others. I've guaranteed you since the starting I would take you home, so I will get you there."

At first, the news didn't sound right. A home? After over an extended period of being out and about? It would be basically impossible. How? The tears that pooled in Evelyn's eyes were confirmation enough. She hadn't sobbed for some things while out and about with her recently discovered family, yet this is totally something to cry about. Not every person finds the opportunity to get back to something a piece of who they used to be. Particularly not something this glory.
Evelyn's body flowed with adrenaline. Goodness, the sweet anguish to stand by just a brief time prior to venturing back on schedule. She got Lily May and conveyed the youngster on her back.

As the gathering made the last stretch to the letter box, they went to one side and up the carport. A white house with blue screens stood gladly before them. She let Lily May down, this time holding the youngster's hand.

The carport was only the manner in which she recollected that it, with the exception of some grass had tracked down its direction through new breaks. Plants ascended the sides of the house, tingling to get in. Evelyn, but enticed to take her shoes off and run through the grass, abstained for now.

A roof over the yard gave the gathering cover as Evelyn fished the key from the hanging blossom crate. When she felt the cool piece of metal in her palm, she cleaned away the soil. Notwithstanding the way that her spirit longed to be in this home finally, Evelyn couldn't resist the opportunity to feel reluctant. This inclination, notwithstanding, is intended for some other time, some other time when her kin aren't remaining vulnerable, ready to be allowed in the house. They documented in individually, all clustered in the entrance as Evelyn shut the entryway behind her.

"Thusly." Evelyn remembered everything. She bumbled for the spotlight in her pack, thankful that another person gave it to her before she let her nerves improve of her. "There are rooms higher up, the children can rest there."

Regardless of the way that there are just four beds, the kids made it work. The grown-ups dozed down the stairs on the love seats and the floor. As the last individual rests for bed, Evelyn couldn't resist the opportunity to feel quiet. She strolled higher up to the workplace, the main accessible room left for her to rest. The floor seemed dusty and cold, something she was utilized to, however something she will change. Her jacket did the trick as a pad regardless of the chill that flowed through her spine. Similarly as she settled in to the point of nodding off, a voice pulled her from her brain.

"Get off the floor." Daniel went after her hands, pulling her up from the beginning. His face held no inclination. A clean canvas.

"I'm in a real sense fine." Evelyn followed him first floor and into the front room. Indeed, she wasn't following him per say, rather being delicately hauled behind him like a little youngster.

Daniel loose into the pads of the little lounge chair, pulling her down with him. His arms encased her like a warm cover. Some portion of her really wanted to feel peculiar dozing close to Daniel. Not in any event, when dozing on the woods floor or in some other safe house did they rest at all near each other. This is the nearest she's consistently been to him.

She rested her hand over his chest and laid her head just beneath his jaw. Evelyn hasn't felt this protected since... all things considered, she was unable to recollect. She likewise didn't recollect nodding off by the same token. The sun was for the most part hindered by the thick drapes, yet it radiated through to a great extent enlightening pieces of the lounge room.

For the first time ever, she didn't need to constrain herself to get up. There is no need. Clearly, the gathering needs to track down food and water, yet rest. Rest is what Evelyn can't get enough of. She cuddled up nearer to Daniel, fearing the second he'll awaken. He resembles a warmer. Much to her dismay he was at that point alert.

The quietness of this nippy early morning finished when the youngsters each of them ten stomped on down the steps like a crowd of elephants. This abrupt explosion of commotion woke the individuals who had been sleeping. Evelyn and Daniel shot up, eyes stripped for risk. He remained behind her, ensuring her back.

"How frequently have we let you know children to be calm when somebody is dozing?" Daniel basically imploded onto the lounge chair. He put his hand over his chest to attempt to quiet his dashing heart.

"I believe they're recently energized." Evelyn murmured.

Daniel gave her a look.

"Let's go." She held her hand out towards him. "We should go check whether the nursery has food."

Everybody followed Evelyn to her granddad's nursery. It seems, by all accounts, to be approaching the finish of its developing season. In any case, there should be sufficient food to last them half a month, perhaps a month. Perhaps more.

Over the course of the morning, everybody split up to gather however much food as could be expected. Crates upon bushels were conveyed up to the house and set on any accessible surface. Evelyn busied herself in the little plantation behind the carport. Four apple trees, one pear tree, and one plum tree. The children helped her, for the most part. The quietness that accompanies an errand as humble as this caused her to feel to some degree typical. It provides Evelyn with a feeling of spot. A required feeling of spot.

"Do you have any containers we could store a portion of this food in?" Daniel moved toward Evelyn with a genuinely enormous bin of corn.

"Perhaps."

He followed her into the house as she took him through the kitchen, following the lounge area, towards a light blue entryway with a metal handle. Evelyn strolled down the wooden steps behind this entryway, snatching an electric lamp from the divider. Straight ahead was the storm cellar sink. Toward her right sat a washer and dryer. To her left side was the clothing rack for wet things. The back divider behind the flight of stairs was fixed with a couple retires, a few wooden cartons, woven containers, and a couple of boxes of containers were left on them.

"There's your response." She pointed the spotlight towards the back divider.

The two of them strolled over to it, pulling down what they were nearest to.

"I never expressed gratitude toward you for thinking that we are this spot." Daniel followed Evelyn back up the means, containers and containers in their grasp.

She set her things on the counter. "You don't have to."

"I truly feel like I ought to. You're an extraordinary pioneer and I'm appreciative for all that you've accomplished for our kin."

Evelyn become flushed. The obscurity of the storm cellar fortunately veiled the redness of her cheeks. "You're an incredible pioneer, as well."

He grinned, chest warming because of her commendation. "Each of the four of us are."

Evelyn promptly imagined the other two innovators to her. Sebastian and Blair. Nonetheless, her psyche remained on Blair. "No doubt, we are. However, i'm worried about Blair."

"I'm, as well. She's not something very similar."

The two of them strolled up the basement steps into the kitchen, setting the provisions on the kitchen counter. Evelyn's eyes looked over the kitchen dividers, halting once they saw a picture of her grandma and granddad. She moaned, sorrowful.

"You alright?" Daniel turned towards her. He saw the anguish in her eyes, lips unhappy in a grimace.

Evelyn shook her head. "I'm so glad to be here, to be home, yet I feel so dismal."

"Come on." Daniel snatched her hand, directing her to a private room higher up. He picked the one toward the finish of the corridor on the left. "Converse with me." They plunked down on the day bed together, unwinding into the bedding. Evelyn didn't have any idea where to begin. Her stomach felt tight, uncomfortable to feel this allowed to talk with Daniel.

"Being back here makes me miss my family." She picked at the skin around her thumb. "The scents, the sounds... they're overpowering. I feel like my heart will break."

Daniel got her hands. "I know."

Evelyn would have rather not cry, however her tears fell before she could take care of them. Her body slouched over in torment. She gripped onto Daniel's hands like they are her life line. It was as of now he maneuvered her into him, holding her head against his chest. Her tears wet his shirt, yet he couldn't have cared less. Daniel would not release her until she quit crying.

"Much obliged to you." She folded her arms over him, thankful for his quality.

"Continuously."

He held her for a brief period longer until she slowed down to rest. Her cheeks dried following a couple of more minutes, and afterward her face quieted from its puffiness.

"Let's go." Daniel gestured towards the entryway. "How about we go follow through with our task."

•••

All of the food from the little nursery and plantation was conveyed up to the kitchen where it was prepared and put away into the containers Evelyn and Daniel found. The food ready to be left out sat in the bins on the kitchen counters, showing up as though they had all returned from a rancher's market. The rest was ready to eat, it would be their first dinner in right around two days.

The youngsters ate first, almost falling into rests once their dinner finished.

"It's OK assuming you folks want to go rest." Daniel saw the dark circles under their eyes. "We have nothing else to do today."

Evelyn paid attention to the retreating strides of ten youngsters. In the wake of completing her feast she understood how parched she had become. She totally neglected to enlighten them regarding the water source on the property.

"There's additionally a river here. I figure we should begin heating up some water." An awkward dryness assumed control over her mouth. She had no question every other person felt dried, as well.

That is by and large what they did. It required hours to bubble and jug sufficient water for the entire gathering. When they had gotten done, it was at that point night. Everyone had an exceptional gleam about them. Something doesn't add up about having a full paunch and clean water that makes a pleasurable high.

Pondering the water they took from the brook helped her to remember the mid year. At whatever point she could, Evelyn would stroll down to the spring shoeless and move down the bank to the water. For a really long time she would attempt to get minnows with a red performance cup. At the point when she had her fill of that, she'd continue on to getting each crayfish she could find.

"Hello, Eve." A more diminutive lady with pale highlights and dull hair drew closer from the lounge room. "I simply needed to say thank you for thinking that we are a spot to remain."

"Harvest time, hello." Evelyn bounced somewhat, having been as far as she could tell. "Try not to stress over it. I'm simply happy I perceived where we were."

"Well if not for you we wouldn't be here the present moment." Just before Autumn went to leave, she immediately folded her arms over Evelyn's shoulders.

"Goodnight." Autumn grinned momentarily prior to strolling back to the front room.

"Night."

Evelyn approached a little gathering of the more youthful children and stooped down to their level. "I simply needed to thank you folks for assisting today. I realize that you've all buckled down and I'm unquestionably glad for you."

"Are we going to live here for some time?" Esma inquired. She is the most seasoned of the kids; just about twelve years.

"We are." Evelyn made a point to give the youngster a splendid grin. "Ideally you'll all be getting new garments soon, and assuming we're fortunate, new beds."

The children became happy very quickly. It's not happy resting in a similar bed as someone else, not to mention four, however they had not dozed in a decent bed for some time. Clean apparel was additionally a victor. A few new shoes, as well, perhaps. Evelyn chose to leave a piece of paper and a pencil with the children, allowing them to record what they think they need.

Evelyn advanced up the steps to the workplace and sat in the PC seat. Her Grandpa used to sit in this seat. Pushing that exceptionally thought from her head, she pulled a yellow scratch pad from the rack over her and started composing a rundown of things the gathering required. One more rundown was made to utilize when counting the food stores. There was such a huge amount to do in what felt like so brief period. In some cases it was not difficult to fail to remember that she has help.

It was an hour prior Evelyn moved from her seat. A large number of records she made of things they expected to endure their first winter as a whole gathering. Was there a method for thinking that it is all? Perhaps. Evelyn thought that it is to some degree entertaining to compose, as she hadn't done as such as far back as she could recall. The handwriting certainly isn't generally so perfect as it used to be, however it took care of business.

"Evie?" A genuinely tall and slender youngster thumped on the door jamb. Evelyn dropped her pencil.

"What's up, Seb?" Evelyn grinned compassionate. She hadn't seen Sebastian in what felt like days.

"So I was contemplating whether there are any stores or places close by that you think may have something that we want?"

She thought briefly. It's been an entire year. There wouldn't be one spot that hasn't been taken advantage of by somebody. Each Walmart, wearing store, and drug store inside a ten mile span would in all likelihood be wiped out. Obviously there are different houses yet there is an enormous possibility they would be vacant too. It was a wonder that this house was left immaculate.

"Perhaps a K-Mart, a Bj's-"

"That is it!" Evelyn bounced from her seat and tossed her arms around Sebastian's shoulders. In no time, her interjection acquired her a little crowd. "So about seven days before the conflict, the BJ's in this town shut as a result of the pandemic. It was leaving business in any case. The specialists boarded the windows and entryways because of a portion of the break-ins that occurred. There's plausible that it wasn't hit as hard as different stores. It's in an unusual area in lacking area and we're a couple of miles from it."

Daniel's head sprung up from behind the entryway. "Tomorrow at the break of day we will look at this spot and check whether it has what we want. We have a ton to do to plan for winter this year."

Sebastian gestured.

"How will we manage the children tomorrow?" Autumn ventured into the workplace with her inquiry, realizing the kids couldn't go with the grown-ups the following day.

"Lets have a gathering about it after we put the children to sleep." Daniel proposed. "I know it's late, yet at this moment we want to zero in on supper."

Everybody concurred and completely finished Daniel's structure. Some more conversation was had at supper over how the dozing game plans would be and who might take stock the following day. It wasn't unfamiliar to have conversations like these, yet it was new to have a rooftop over their heads and full guts. Meaning it is new to have this conversation in the security of a home. However, it feels decent.

Every youngster was not long after taken care of with the arrangement that they would be joined by somebody after their watchmen had their gathering.

"Evelyn, how can we go to go with regards to tomorrow?" Daniel inquired. His unemotional face basically gazed into her spirit while his edge overshadowed her. "You realize this region better than any of us."

She does. A big part of the town is engrained into her memory. Perhaps this could be a fresh start for everybody. A new beginning.

"In particular, the children need to remain here and I figure five or six of us should remain behind." Evelyn pulled the rundowns she made before from her jacket pocket. "We want a huge load of stuff to endure this colder time of year and we want to finish a great deal of stuff before the primary ice. Tomorrow on our run we can discuss the points of interest of the things we want to find, however at the present time we really want to zero in on the general strategy.

I really want one pioneer to remain here with three or four others to look after the children, assemble food, and gather water. Myself and three or four others will walk about a few miles to get to Bj's." Evelyn held everybody's consideration as she portrayed what expected to happen the following day.

"What might be said about over the long haul?" Autumn played with the closures of her dull hair. "What will we want to do here to make due through the colder time of year?"

"Well," Evelyn began. "Somebody should be doled out to making more retires to place in the cellar and we really want to assemble an expansion to the house for additional rooms. We want a couple of latrines and perhaps a shower."

"I could construct the racks for later." Blair shouted out. "I could likewise draw up certain plans for different conveniences assuming you'd like?"

"That would be extremely valuable, and you're free to involve any of the devices in the carport. There's a huge load of additional wood in the room joined to the carport you can use also. Key is on the divider in the kitchen." Evelyn felt like things were at long last meeting up. Everybody had such countless inquiries, maybe the gathering continued for quite a long time. Much to their dismay that the "resting" kids got each word. In recalling the previous year had been the hardest any of them had at any point confronted, they each felt committed to take care of their gatekeepers. Particularly after all that their gatekeepers had accomplished for them.

The day had passed by faster than Evelyn could grasp. Once more, she imparts the lounge chair to Daniel, with the exception of this time the two of them lay on their sides, her back against his chest and his arm around her abdomen. Try not to misunderstand her, she cherishes nestles, however there's a stupendous thing about having one's own bed.

Obviously, she shouldn't say anything negative. Assuming that they had kept strolling for significantly longer the other way they likely wouldn't have viewed as a home. Very few individuals, of those that are left, can encounter something like this these days. A rooftop over their head. Food. Water. Family.

Her eyes shut, however her cerebrum stayed alert and ready to go. Recollections hued themselves to her, showing particular individuals or spots exposed by what she encountered today. She could see her folks, her kin. Her old pets showed up or two. Ideally, any place they are, they're alright. That is all Evelyn could expect. Hot tears trickled over the extension of her nose, wetting the texture of the love seat against her cheek. She wouldn't dare move either, best not to upset anybody.

It was the instability of her body that pulled Daniel from his rest. It was the one thing she was unable to control. His hand dropped down her arm, at long last binding his fingers through hers. She quit moving.

Daniel then, at that point, prodded Evelyn to turn and face him. She moved as discreetly as could be expected, realizing that the springs in this old love seat can be unforgiving. They lay chest to chest now, temples contacting, gazing at one another with the assistance of the bits of twilight not held under control by the draperies. He was unable to do much in the method of words, so he picked to maneuvering her head into his chest. He felt her arm fold over his side, the other grasped into her chest.

Evelyn cried quietly for her family until her body could never again remain alert. Daniel clutched her even in his own rest. They didn't move for the remainder of the evening.

•••

Promptly the following morning Evelyn set herself up. Not just for the run she was going to lead, yet for the fate of her kin. To her it seems like such a lot of lays on her shoulders. Once in a while that overloads her, however not today.

As she wrapped tying up her shoelaces, her fringe got the figures of Daniel and Sebastian. She remained from her seat and moved toward them.

"Do both of you want to accompany me today?"

Sebastian gestured, a huge smile all the rage. "What sort of inquiry is that? Obviously I need to accompany you."

Daniel just raised an eyebrow. His arms crossed before him. "I mean somebody needs to ensure you don't step aerobics a bear trap once more."

"Dude..." Sebastian frowned at Daniel. He recollected that day like no other. Evelyn's shout pierced his spirit and broke his heart. The cold of the metal stung his skin when he liberated her from the snare. Talk about a center memory.

"It's alright, Seb." Evelyn grinned tenderly. "Be prepared in ten. I need to talk with Blair before we leave."

Apologies

"Hey, Blair?" Evelyn reached out to grab the shorter girl's arm. Blair pulled away. Despite being taken aback, Evelyn continued to speak. "I just wanted to let you know that if you run out of any materials, you can go to the neighbors house across the street. They might still have extra lumber."

"Okay." With only the singular word being said, Blair turned and left. What is her deal?

Evelyn has to focus on her trip to BJ's. She has to focus on the future of the youngest group members. The future of her people. Her future. Now is not the time to be hurt by some stupid reaction. She decided she would fix it later.

"You ready?" Evelyn's thoughts were interrupted by an eager Sebastian. He smiled brightly, ready to get the day started.

"I think so." Evelyn responded faintly. "I'm a little nervous, I'm not gonna lie."

"Don't worry about that," Sebastian pauses to hand her a backpack, and then continues: "because you grew up around here and you have us. You're not alone."

Although Sebastian's reassurance was helpful, it wasn't the true reason why Evelyn felt so anxious. She couldn't help but think about Blair's reaction towards being touched. Maybe she is just one of those types of people that doesn't like physical contact, and that's okay. That, on top of the stress of hopefully finding the things her group needs, was enough to make Evelyn want to stay home. To fix things.

She must've overstepped boundaries. That was probably it. Maybe if she—

"Eve. Sebastian." Daniel approached Sebastian and Evelyn.

"Hey, Danny." Evelyn tightened the straps of her pack, immediately brought back to the memory of him consoling her last night.

He acted like it never happened.

"So," Daniel began. "I found someone to come with us who's willing to help with some heavy lifting."

As soon as those words were spoken, the fourth member of this small scavenging group appeared in the circle. It was Fox, a previous offensive lineman for their college.

"Hey, guys!" Fox smiled and waved. The one thing Evelyn always loved about him is that his teeth are so white they're almost blinding.

"Good morning, Fox." Evelyn grinned, welcoming his cheeriness into her heart. He is one of the kindest people she's ever known. "Let's head out guys. We have a lot to do today."

Before leaving, Daniel made sure to tell the other leader—Blair, who stayed behind, that himself and his three companions would be gone for most of the morning and would return in the early afternoon at the latest.

Evelyn watched her friends walk to the road and wondered where they were going. "Guys!" They turned to meet her gaze. "You're going the wrong way." She pointed to the creek.

"You're kidding, right?" Sebastian looked to Evelyn in disbelief. The creek? Is she serious?

"No, Seb." Evelyn laughed and she shook her head. "We have to cross this creek and then walk in a straight line up the hill for about two and a half miles."

"Up the hill?" Sebastian looked hilariously pained. Maybe some extra cardio would be good for him.

"If it makes you feel any better, it's all downhill when we come back." Evelyn covered her mouth to hide her laughter.

"I guess so." Sebastian sighed and began to trudge through

the frigid water.
"Why can't we just take the road?" Daniel, just like Sebastian, wanted absolutely nothing to do with walking through the creek.
Evelyn recalled that most of the townsfolk were old and are most likely dead or gone, but she didn't know if her and her people would be the only ones in this town. "I don't want to risk us running into other people."
"But the water, though." Daniel seemed adamant about taking any path that didn't involve trekking through a frigid creek. To some extent Evelyn understands, but she'd rather go through the woods unseen than the middle of the road with houses flanking both sides. She would not risk the safety of the children.
Evelyn stopped walking, staring down Daniel. They both stood facing each other, shin deep in the water. Fox and Sebastian waited on the bank.
"Do you wanna take us to the BJ's since my way of travel isn't good enough for you?" She has no problem standing up to him.
Daniel didn't say anything. His unresponsive face stared down at Evelyn. He turned to follow Sebastian and Fox to the edge of the bank, leaving Evelyn by herself in the water.
"Nope. I'm good."
It wasn't necessarily the worst when walking through the creek, it was having to deal with wet feet and ankles the entire way to the BJ's. The weather didn't make it too terrible, though. For one, they couldn't risk running into other people, especially now that they have a home. A little cold water wouldn't hurt. Being occupied by conversation made the time pass quicker.
"Hey guys?" Evelyn debated on whether or not she should ask her question. "Have any of you noticed anything off about Blair today?"
The boys were silent for a moment.
"She seemed like her normal self to me." Sebastian shrugged, shaking some extra water from his boots.

"I thought she was a little quieter than normal, but other than that Blair seemed fine." Daniel replied. "Why?"
"Before we left I tried to talk with her, but she was acting strange." Evelyn frowned. "I just hope she's alright."
The boys hoped so too, even Fox.
"What about you, Fox?" Daniel gently elbowed his friend. "Aren't you two as thick as thieves?"
"Yeah..." Fox appeared lost in his head. "I noticed her behavior, too. I know that she talked with Autumn before I did. Maybe it was something Autumn said?"
No one knew.
"We can figure out later when we get back," Daniel adjusted the backpack on his shoulders, "but for now I think we should focus on what to expect when we get to BJ's."
Daniel is right. There's no point in distracting oneself when there are important matters to take care of. With this in mind, the four traveled the last half an hour with ease. They only talked about subjects that would keep their heads focused on the task at hand.
Once they made it to the top of the hill, their gaze locked on the back of the BJ's. They made it. They are out of breath, but they made it. All four took a second to collect themselves, then they boys followed Evelyn around the front and helped her take down the boards covering the doors. They stepped inside and grabbed flashlights from the bin on the cashiers table. Only two worked, but it was still light nonetheless.
"Everything is still here." Evelyn looked at all of the cardboard boxes on the ground. Some are still open, others are shut. It looked like the people that worked here stopped packing halfway through. It made sense given that the war was only a few days later.
"From the looks of it, there's gonna be more here than we can carry." Daniel analyzed all of the shelves and racks. "But we'll get what we need first before anything that we want."
Everyone split up, Evelyn going to the clothing section and

the boys going elsewhere. Evelyn pulled so many clothing items from the racks and stuffed them in her backpack. There was no way she'd be able to take home enough clothes for everyone. Then an idea hit her. She took her flashlight and started searching through the other aisles.
"Hey, Evie!" Sebastian greeted her. He held multiple storage bins in his hands.
"I'm actually glad I ran into you." Evelyn grinned almost Cheshire-like. "I'm gonna need to steal one of those bins from you, if you don't mind."
"Sure! That's totally fine." Sebastian gave her a bin and a lid. "Did you find what you were looking for?"
Evelyn nodded. Her eyes canvassed the shelves around her. This sight feels almost normal. Nostalgia brewed in the pit of her stomach. She looked back to Sebastian before she could become too saddened.
"Yes. You wouldn't believe how much stuff just didn't get packed up." Evelyn turned to leave. "Thanks, Sebby."
"It's no problem."
Evelyn walked back to the clothing section and began pulling things from the racks. In order to save space she rolled everything and packed it tightly. It took maybe half an hour, but she managed to fill the tub with clothing for everyone. Both the kids and the adults. After doing so, she pushed the bin to the front doors and met up with Sebastian again. It was heavier than she thought.
"Could you spare another bin?" Evelyn twisted her fingers.
"Anything for you, Eve." Sebastian handed over another. "Would you like some help with finding the right sized shoes?"
It didn't seem like a bad idea.
"That would be greatly appreciated." Evelyn walked by his side to where the shoes were located. "We only need twenty pairs."
"That's a lot of shoes."
"Tell me about it."
This time, it didn't take nearly as long to fill the bin up with

shoes, but it was certainly much heavier than the bin with the clothes. Both Evelyn and Sebastian wondered how they would carry these bins back to their home. They would find a way. They always have.
"How are you guys doing?" Fox approached them with a trolley and a wide grin.
"Where did you find that!?" Sebastian laughed out loud. This trolley is the solution.
"It was in the back, Daniel is back there right now getting a few more." Fox lifted the bin of shoes onto the trolley and walked with his friends to the front of the store. As he lifted the bin of clothes onto the trolley, he continued to speak. "Not only that, but I found plenty of bed frames and mattresses. Enough for all of us."
With all of this in mind, it is much easier to imagine a future for the whole group. Everything they need is right here in front of them. This is the first time they've ever hit a supply jackpot.
"Alright guys," Daniel pulled two trolleys behind him. "I'm gonna grab one more trolley and some tie downs so we can take our stuff back without having to carry it. Evie, is there a road we can take back to the house?"
"Yes, there is."
Daniel nodded and left. Evelyn thought of a plan.
"Let's keep like items with like items. It'll be easier in the long run." Evelyn pointed to where on the trolleys their findings would fit best.
"I agree with you." Fox helped lift more plastic boxes of items onto the trolley. "Although, I want to push the heaviest one."
"That's fine." Evelyn nodded. She would rather have Fox push it than her. "We won't have to worry about too much hill on the way back, the road has a slight decline."
"Is there anything left on that list of yours, Eve?" Sebastian read through it one more time. "We got the clothes and shoes, beds, extra comforters and sheets, pillows."
Sebastian checked off relatively each item from the list, it

seemed like they'd gotten most of what was needed. Of course, they couldn't get everything. They would need to make another trip. For now, what they had found is enough. It is more than enough.

Before the four left, they made sure to strap down everything to each trolley and board the doors back up. Evelyn locked the doors before the last board was put back.

"I didn't realize how heavy this was going to be." Evelyn stretched her sore hands. They'd been walking for a while now.

"Do you want to take a break?" Daniel's arms strained, too.

"You should probably ask Fox, he's pushing the heaviest one." She replied.

"Nah, thanks though." Fox seemed to be doing fine.

"Well, you'll all be happy to know that we've got about five minutes left until we reach home." Evelyn expressed a faint smile, nearly out of breath. Each man exclaimed in happiness, almost driven by a new kind of energy. They had to conserve it, though.

Evelyn could feel her lungs constricting. The cold air only worsened her condition. Black spots began to speckle her vision. She cursed internally.

The last five minutes felt like it dragged on forever, but the driveway is now in sight. The sound of the trolleys on the pavement attracted the attention from those in the house. They came rushing outside to help their friends.

"How was it?"

"How did the trip go?"

"You guys brought back so much..."

The other six college students gave the four a break. Evelyn swayed. The black dots swarmed like bees this time. Dehydration is not a move.

"Hey," Blair steadied Evelyn, "let me take over."

Evelyn was taken aback yet again. Not only had Blair spoken to her, she reached out to her. Almost like this morning never happened. First it was Daniel, and now Blair. What's happening?

"Blair?" Evelyn's voice stopped Blair in her tracks. "Are you okay?"

"I am now." Blair took the trolley to the house and left Evelyn to have a moment to herself.

What did Blair mean? Evelyn had no clue. Maybe she would ask.

"Come on, Evie." Daniel waved her over. They walked together up to the house and sat down on the porch together. "You looked like you were about to pass out back there."

"If I looked it, then I probably was." Evelyn rested her head in the palms of her hands, completely exhausted. "Thanks for the help."

"You've got to stop thanking me." Daniel smiled ever so slightly. "It's what friends are for."

Friends?

Evelyn wasn't sure about friends. More like comrades? They hadn't had one conversation about something not having to do with their people or finding ways to keep themselves alive. Well, he did console her when she revealed her feelings about being back in her childhood home. Does that count as friendship, though? Honestly, it's too much to think about at the moment.

"Come on," Evelyn stood, feeling somewhat better, "let's get something to eat."

Daniel took her hand, but put none of his weight behind it. Evelyn grew to be quite exhausted for something of that manner. Daniel knew that, of course. They followed their friends inside to the kitchen and grabbed some water and a plate full of food, then sat down next to Fox and Sebastian.

"How are you guys doing?" Fox asked, taking a large bite of his corn.

Sebastian feels fine. Energized even.

"Decent." Daniel then looked over to Evelyn. "How about you Evie?"

Evelyn picked her head up from the table and sighed. "I'm existing."

Sebastian chuckled. Fox grinned. As expected, Daniel rolled his eyes.

"What? It's true!" She exclaimed. Evelyn isn't nearly as strong as Daniel or Sebastian, let alone Fox, but she managed well enough on her own.

"Next time you're going to carry a little less." Sebastian scolded. "Each time I looked at you, your face was as white as a sheet."

"Hey!" Evelyn's jaw dropped. "I was perfectly capable of doing it myself."

"That's not what I said." Sebastian held up a finger, making it clear he would never intentionally belittle her.

The guys shook their heads and continued to eat, knowing very well that Evelyn is incredibly strong. She only used a little too much of her energy. Getting the chance to actually sit down and eat in a chair feels incredible, though. Another level of relaxation kind of incredible.

"Hey, Evelyn?" Blair approached her friends. Evelyn paused her conversation, a smile on her cheeks. "Could you come take a walk with me for a second?"

"Yeah." Evelyn rose from her seat and excused herself. Blair led Evelyn to the basement. They took the stairs down together. "Is there something you need to talk about?"

"I actually want to talk to you about a few things." Blair turned on her solar-powered flashlight. It shone against three sets of shelves that set against the wall. All of the canned foods from the day before were organized perfectly on each shelf.

"Blair..." Evelyn grazed her hand over each individual shelf. "This is amazing!"

"Thank you. I was hoping you'd like—" Blair was interrupted by a pair of arms that wrapped around her shoulders.

"I love them. Thank you." Evelyn pulled back, grateful for the new shelves, but also reprimanding herself for crossing Blair's boundaries again. She then turned to admire the shelves some more. "I actually wanted to talk to you about some things as well. Come with me?"

Evelyn walked up to the second floor with Blair close behind. They entered the first bedroom.

"This room used to be two. I was hoping you'd know how to build a wall to separate it again. Would that be possible?" Evelyn hoped her request is within Blair's skill set.

"Of course I can. I could build you a house if you wanted." Blair surprised herself by her own words, despite meaning every single one of them.

"We will get to that later." Evelyn smiled. They then moved to the other bedrooms down the hall. "These two bedrooms use to be one whole room. This middle wall isn't a supporting wall, and I was hoping you could turn these two rooms into three?"

"I can do that." Blair studied both rooms. "I'll draw up plans immediately. Is there anything else you need from me?"

"Yeah, actually. Let's talk in the office." Evelyn waved her over to a chair and they sat down together. "I think it's super important that we build an addition to the garage. It would create extra living space for the kids and us, and the addition is technically already there, it's just unfinished."

"Is this addition currently accessible?" Blair wanted to know exactly how much work she'd need to put into this addition.

"Yes, there's a finished set of stairs and floor above. It spans the entire garage, including the studio room on the ground level."

"Could you maybe take me there now?"

They walked together with the garage keys in hand. This is kind of exciting. It had been at least two years since Evelyn had gone up to the addition, and she couldn't help but be thrilled to share this space with someone else. She opened the studio door and went up the stairs. To her left appeared a large space. On the floor sat hundreds of planks of wood, each one collecting dust.

"This is incredible." Blair counted ten skylights and seven

windows. There looked to be more than enough wood to build what Evelyn needed her to build. "I'm gonna get on those plans right away. This is so cool."

"I'm glad you think so." Evelyn smiled and handed the shorter girl a notebook. "This is yours to use. You're welcome to the studio downstairs as well, and if you want you can build onto it however you like."

"Thank you." Blair didn't know how to thank Evelyn. "I won't let you down."

"I know."

Evelyn walked back down the stairs, leaving Blair to her devices. Before she could get far, her name was called.

"Eve..." Blair picked at the dried skin around her fingernails. "I am sorry for the way I acted towards you this morning. I shouldn't have reacted the way I did."

"I know you're sorry, and I'm sorry for pushing boundaries." Evelyn sat down on the stairs and faced Blair. "I could tell something was wrong, but I didn't want to push you."

"It won't happen again. I promise." Blair looked into Evelyn's eyes, almost hesitant to do so.

"You know you can talk to me, right?" Evelyn reassured.

Blair sat down next to her, feeling a little more comfortable. "I know."

With everything that needed to be said, said, Evelyn left the garage and joined the others. She watched all of the children kick around a partially deflated soccer ball in the backyard. It brought her this happiness she hasn't felt in such a long time. A few of the college kids brought some more food up from the garden. They waved to Evelyn, one handing her a couple strawberries.

"Hey, I was hoping I could talk to you about the sleeping arrangements." It was none other than Autumn who approached Evelyn.

"What about them?" Evelyn remembered what Fox said earlier this morning.

"I know that she talked with Autumn before I did. Maybe it

was something that Autumn said?"
"You guys were able to bring back, like, twelve beds. Would we be able to make enough room for all of them?" Autumn seemed to want her own bed.
"I can make room for three extra beds upstairs and two in the living room, but that's all the space we have." There wasn't much Evelyn could do. "Until the addition over the garage is completed, I'm afraid we will have to make do with what we have."
"Addition?" Autumn looked perplexed. Then it hit Evelyn, she never told anyone.
"I need to call a meeting." She has to tell everyone immediately, and began stressfully munching on her strawberries. "Please round up everyone that you can and tell them to meet me in the living room."
Autumn went off to do exactly as Evelyn requested. The leader walked up to the house and gathered the rest of her people. Once everyone had arrived, she began to speak.
"I talked with Blair earlier about building a few things for us, and she is currently drawing up some plans to create a total of five bedrooms above us, and some extra bedrooms above the garage." Evelyn took this pause to sit in a chair, eating her last strawberry. Her exhaustion began to get the better of her. "By the looks of it, I believe that every single one of us will be able to have a room of our own. Now, this process will take a few weeks but we need to help Blair as much as we can. This project needs to be completed before winter sets in."
"What do you suggest the kids do?" Fox wanted to make sure the children didn't feel left out.
"I'm glad you asked." Evelyn had though about this earlier. "During the construction part of each room, we will use eight of the ten of us adults. Two of us will act as instructors for some of the kids. A select few of the children can help with the smaller jobs involved with building onto the addition. This way everyone has something to be a part of."
"I like it." Daniel nodded in agreement.

Evelyn continued her speech. "Blair is going to spend the rest of the afternoon making blueprints for the addition, and hopefully we will start construction within the week."
A new sense of hope flooded through the hearts of everyone in the room. This place is on its way to becoming their home.
As soon as everyone went back to what they were doing before the meeting started, Evelyn decided to check on Blair. Maybe bring her some lunch? She started up the steps once more and watched the architect scribble in her new notebook. It was a very interesting sight. Her back was turned to the stairs, her mind lost in her new project. Quietly, Evelyn set the plate down on the floor and placed the glass of water beside it. She didn't want to disturb Blair, no, but at the same time Evelyn wanted to be in her presence. Without making a sound, Evelyn tiptoed back down the stairs.
"You can stay if you'd like." Blair looked happily at Evelyn. "I don't mind the company."
Evelyn blushed and walked towards the plate of food she set on the floor, picked it and the glass of water up, and handed them to Blair.
"So how's the plan coming along?" Evelyn wanted to see if there were any sketches to look at yet.
"It's actually going smoother than expected. The way these windows and skylights are spaced gives me enough room to design an area for exactly twelve bedrooms. Six on each wall with a hallway in the middle." Blair showed Evelyn her sketches. "In this final rough draft sketch I was able to comfortably fit twelve smaller rooms in this formation so that each room either gets a window or a skylight."
"This is brilliant." Evelyn looked from the mathematical equations to the beautiful, plan-view sketches. At least they are beautiful to her, to Blair not so much. "It's also not like we need twenty rooms. We have a few couples among us."
"With the five bedrooms I hope to build in the house, that brings us to a total of seventeen rooms. This is more than

enough for us all." Blair emanated proudness. Never had she come up with a design that made her as happy as this one. "I was also thinking of converting half of the studio downstairs into a bedroom for myself, but I didn't want to just in case you want that area preserved."
Evelyn felt touched. That studio did belong to her late Grandfather. He used it for his professional photography business. It held so many special memories, but she knew the potential it carried for so many more. Evelyn trusted Blair.
"You have my permission, and I appreciate your thoughtfulness." Evelyn smiled happily, remembering her beloved Grandfather. "I know you'll create something beautiful."
"Thank you, Eve." Blair reached over her empty plate of food and squeezed Evelyn tightly.
"No, thank you." Evelyn hugged her back.
•••
Back in the house, Daniel helped take some of the food down into the basement. He busied himself with this until the sky grew a little darker than it was before he entered the basement. As he turned to leave, the sight of another person in the room made him jump. He thought he was alone up until this point.
"You know you could've knocked or something." Daniel ignored the palpitations in his heart.
Evelyn grimaced, feeling guilty for scaring him. "I didn't mean to startle you."
"Mhm."
Evelyn opened her mouth to rebuttal, but no words came out. Daniel's gaze remained permanently fixated on her. She couldn't escape. Her heart pounded at an uncontrollable rate. Is he going to say something?
"How's your ankle?" He glanced down at it, remembering the blood that poured from the once open wound.
Evelyn sighed, tired of his prodding. Her fingers squeezed the bridge of her nose. "You know Daniel, I've had it up to

here with your—"
"I'm being genuine."
He didn't quite like hearing his full first name. Especially from her mouth.
Evelyn was stunned to silence. A few seconds passed before she could coherently respond. Not once has he asked her about her injury. This would be the first time. Why, though, is he asking her now? Why didn't he ask her when it healed?
"It's okay..." Her eyes dropped to her ankle. "Sometimes it hurts, but it's fine."
Daniel nodded. Leaving the basement without further conversation, leaving Evelyn quite perplexed. What an odd interaction.
She left the basement after collecting herself. Her mind couldn't quite wrap itself around their conversation despite its simplicity. Even during dinner she was disconnected. Stuck in her mind. The mealtime passed quickly, as did the rest of the day. Darkness enveloped the house once all of the candles were put out.
Evelyn lay on the couch by herself, shivering. Her shoes came off earlier and sit by the other end of the couch. Daniel still hasn't come back from being outside. One of the children had to relieve themselves. In the meantime she pulled a blanket around her body in hopes it would provide her with some kind of insulation. It didn't do much, but it's better than nothing. She pressed her back flat against the back of the couch, wishing to retain some heat. Her nose buried itself into the thin blanket.
Daniel entered the house, taking off his shoes by the door. The child with him ran up the stairs to their bed. After maneuvering himself around some of the bodies asleep on the floor, he made it safely to the couch he and Evelyn share. The darkness surrounding them couldn't conceal her shivers. Her frame shook, but not enough to make the couch springs protest. However, they groaned under the additional weight of a second body. Daniel crawled under

the blanket next to Evelyn, both facing each other.
Daniel pulled Evelyn into him despite her frigid fingers and nose. His arms wrapped around her back and held tight. Relaxation settled into her muscles as the warmth lulled her to sleep. Daniel couldn't sleep just yet, though. His mind wandered to the memory of Evelyn getting stuck in the bear trap. It was a miracle she survived.
He remembered holding onto her as Sebastian pulled the trap away from her ankle. They had to stay put for a while after she got hurt. Daniel allowed himself to sleep knowing he would never allow her to be hurt again.

The Chill of the Night

"His asthma is beginning to get awful." Marcy murmured towards Evelyn. "I don't have the foggiest idea what to do."

Marcy observed agonizingly as her sweetheart Graham attempted to relax. A perceptible wheeze reverberated off the exposed dividers of the room. She enclosed her hands by his, trusting somebody would figure out how to work on his condition.

"There is a drug store uptown. I'll go on a run today to think that he is an inhaler." Evelyn guaranteed the couple that she would put forth a valiant effort to track down Graham something to facilitate his manifestations.

Ground floor she loaded herself a little pack with a filtered water. She informed whoever she ran into of her arrangements, then, at that point, left the glow of her new home. The freshness of the natural air filled her lungs and almost stung her eyes.

"Where are you going?"

Evelyn's look locked on to Daniel. He moved toward her with his sleeves moved up and perspire flickering on his forehead. She generally overlooks the tattoo sleeve covering his arm.

"On a rush to the drug store." She gestured her head in its overall bearing. "Graham needs an inhaler."

"Isn't Sebastian currently on a run?"

"Aren't you expected to assist Blair with building the expansion?" Evelyn folded her arms over her chest.

Daniel's glare was adequately strong enough to make a spike in Evelyn's mindfulness. She watched him roll down his sleeves and shrug on the coat he had already tied around his hips.

"Just shut up and allow me to accompany you."

Evelyn held up her hands in give up. "Essentially let another person know you're leaving with me." She trusted that Daniel will return, watching the leaves tumble from the trees. As they drifted to the ground the sun would get them at a point, making a more energetic shading. She wanted to paint it.

"You prepared?" Daniel strolled down the front advances, throwing a beanie in Evelyn's lap.

"I've been prepared."

Daniel thought back behind him, raising an eyebrow because of her nerve. After practically exceeding all expectations and not having any desire to make a bonehead of himself, Daniel took cues from Evelyn. Sometimes he would sneak a look at her, however just when he realized she wasn't looking. Neither of them said a word for a large portion of the excursion. It was distinctly towards the end when Evelyn shouted out.

"Danny..."

"Hm."

She would truly not like to inquire. "I don't need you to misinterpret this, yet for what reason would you say you are making a special effort to converse with me and be with me?"

"Am I not permitted to?"

"That is not what I'm talking about." Evelyn was uncertain of how to appropriately word her sentiments. "To the furthest extent that I can recollect, you and I have never been close. Not even at school. You've addressed me more and have invested more energy with me in the beyond couple of days than you have in the last, similar to, four years."

Daniel said nothing. He couldn't sort out some way to react. What would he be able to say that sounds conceivable if possible?

"You're not difficult to associate with." Daniel shrugged his shoulders. His hands tracked down their direction into his pockets. "I additionally like conversing with you."

Evelyn nearly couldn't hear his last assertion, yet she did. "Who are you and how have you managed Daniel?"

This glare is not normal for some other. It holds onto one's spirit most awfully. It ventures into the profundities of the psyche. In the speediest design it can impart dread, however not on Evelyn. She's safe. On many event she has encountered each and every glare. She would snicker, however this present time isn't the opportunity.

"I'm simply joking." Evelyn tenderly knock her shoulder against his bicep. She was unable to determine what sort of temperament Daniel is in. His face is void all of the time of demeanor.

"How much longer?"

Evelyn feigned exacerbation, her fun loving tone gone immediately. "We're here."

The structure shows up little outwardly, however feels somewhat greater when inside. The entryway is locked, yet it didn't prevent her from breaking one of the glass sheets. She contacted her hand inside and opened the entryway. As she ventured through the edge, doing great to stay away from the wrecked glass on the wooden floor, her eyes directed her to the counter toward the back. The light from the windows is to the point of enlightening the dusty room.

A debilitated pleasant smell attacked her noses. "What is that?"

"Presumably a dead creature."

Evelyn didn't appreciate it. She moved over the counter and bounced down on the floor. The impact point of her foot got on something, almost stumbling her simultaneously. She got herself on one of the racks before her, thinking back to see what entangled her. She wheezed, a hand over her mouth. The dead storekeeper lay decaying on the ground with an unfilled pill bottle in his grasp.

"Are you alright?!" Daniel quickly jumped over the counter, racing to her side. His eyes followed to the cadaver, frowning at the sight. He thought back to Evelyn who confronted away from it.

She wouldn't move from her spot.

"Where are the inhalers?" Daniel wouldn't walk out on her until she reacted.

She could point.

Similarly as Daniel went to look, Evelyn locked onto his coat. He quit moving and directed his concentration toward her.

"Assist me with looking." He realizes where it counts Evelyn would rather not be left alone with the body.

As they stepped before the overall region she highlighted, Evelyn came to the most noteworthy rack and pulled down a few little boxes. Daniel took them from her hands and dropped them into her knapsack. They left the drug store quickly, keeping away from the dead man on the floor. Right when Evelyn got a much needed refresher she separated. Tears obfuscated her vision. Her hands adjusted on her knees as she frantically attempted to slow down and rest, yet it wouldn't come to her.

Daniel has been conversing with her this entire time, however she was unable to hear his words. The main thing her psyche would permit her to focus on is the memory of the cadaver. She imploded. Free hair got away from her mesh and hung before her tear-stained face.

Daniel bowed before Evelyn. He brushed her hair out of her face, putting it behind her ears. "Slow, full breaths."

She could hear him this time.

"Control it."

Evelyn kept a consistent cadence subsequent to bombing the initial not many occasions, just taking in through her nose and out through her mouth. The adrenaline blurred after some time and her body loose. She cleared the removes from her face, getting up starting from the earliest stage Daniel's assistance.

"Did you know him?"

Evelyn gestured.

Daniel painstakingly folded his arm over her. "How about we return home."

At the point when they got back, Sebastian was at that point in the kitchen planning lunch. He obviously returned only minutes before Evelyn and Daniel who separated once inside the house. She gave Marcy the inhalers for Graham while Daniel went to talk with Sebastian concerning what occurred on their run.

"Is she OK?" Sebastian worriedly bit on his food.

"She had a fit of anxiety, however she's improving." Daniel watched her from far off. She right now sits with a portion of the children. They're showing her a game they made up.

"Much obliged for telling me."

"Try also this to her." Daniel cautioned Sebastian. "I need her to tell you all alone."

Sebastian heaved, went along with that Daniel would even think Sebastian unequipped for being wary. "She's my closest companion. I know the proper behavior around her."

With this said, they headed out in different directions.

Evelyn kept herself occupied the remainder of the evening by assisting Blair with building the expansion. She lost count of the number of nails she pounded into the wooden sheets throughout recent hours. This interruption held a specific memory under control.

"You OK?" Sebastian moved to remain close to Evelyn. "You appear to be not quite right."

Evelyn didn't know where to start. "I don't have any idea." His eyebrows wrinkled and his lips discouraged into a scowl. "You couldn't say whether you're okay?"

Everything she could do is shrug.

"We should talk later. Is that OK?"

Sebastian gestured and left it at that.

Supper drew closer similarly as. Everybody lounged around with a plate of food in their grasp. The kids discussed what all they achieved inside the day and what they anticipate tomorrow. The grown-ups didn't talk about a lot other than the past. Evelyn left the room once she completed the process of eating. She said her goodnights and shut herself away in the workplace higher up. At this time she permitted herself to separate. Recollections overwhelmed her brain from before when the world was ordinary. Everything made herextremely upset.

A particular thump on the entryway stopped Evelyn's cries. She cleaned her face and took a full breath.

"Come in."

Sebastian. He shut the entryway behind him and inclined toward the work area before her. In just an issue of a subsequent he saw the redness in her eyes and the puffiness under her lashes. Her breathing has a specific hiccup in it simply referred to occur because of one specific occasion.

"You realize you can cry before me." Sebastian cleaned away a double crossing tear. "What happened today?"

Evelyn gazed toward him. She attempted frantically to hold herself together, yet was fruitless. When their eyes met her head dropped, and many tears with it. Some portion of her would have rather not face what she saw. She prepared herself against the work area.

"Inhale." Sebastian got down on his knees, level with Evelyn. His left hand scoured her back while his right held firmly to one of her hands. "Gradually."

Evelyn did as Sebastian delicately instructed. Their temples contacted once she had the option to quiet herself. At the point when she was prepared to talk, he tuned in.

"We went to the drug store for inhalers for Graham after you left." Evelyn breathed in profoundly, proceeding with once the shake in her voice dispersed. "I used to work there..."

"I recall you letting me know that when we initially became companions."

Evelyn could gesture. "We strolled in. It smelled entertaining. Daniel said it was a dead creature."

Sebastian knew with this last explanation where her story is going.

"It wasn't." He murmured. "It was your old chief, wasn't it."

She gestured, new tears in her eyes. "How'd you know?"

"You used to discuss him a great deal. I came to an obvious conclusion."

After her admission they sat peacefully, embracing. They stand presently, completely encompassed in one another's arms. Evelyn's ear squeezes right on top of Sebastian's heart. The musical pounding hushing her into a more quiet state. He holds her head against his chest and rests his jaw on. His other hand rubs circles over her back.

"Much obliged to you." Evelyn wraps her arms more tight around his abdomen.

"Try not to say thanks to me." He kissed the highest point of her head. "I'm here all the time for you."

•••

Not long before bed, the remainder of the kids documented into the house in the wake of mitigating themselves. Graham and Marcy appropriated one of the higher up rooms with the goal that he may recuperate all the more without any problem. Each of the youngsters dozed in the other two rooms. The other grown-ups rested in the lounge room.

Evelyn was the final remaining one up once more. She imparted the sofa to Daniel. He previously lay sleeping soundly. How he could get it done? They saw exactly the same thing. A similar dead man. Envy thundered under her skin.

She turned over, her back to him. The glow of the sweeping was to the point of helping her while heading to rest.

Birds flew about the blue sky untethered by the tasks of human existence. Evelyn respects this. Their crude capacity to be a piece of something so regular and delightful, yet likewise destroying and dismal on occasion attracted her. The inclination is unexplainable.

"We're here." Evelyn ventured over the limit of the drug store with alert. She wouldn't need broken glass stuck on her shoes.

She saw the counter towards the back and strolled to it. Effortlessly she jumped it and landed securely on the ground. She pivoted with the inclination that something was watching her, however when she did her eyes just met Daniel's. No other person's. The floor, in any case, was covered with void pill bottles. Similarly as Evelyn turned around to look the racks, she encountered the decaying body of her old chief. It menacingly overshadowed her, the strong strands of skin and muscle hanging a simple inch before her face. The odor attacked her noses, turning into the main thing she could smell. Her environmental factors blurred, and Daniel with them.

Her body froze in dread.

Evelyn woke up shrouded in sweat. She glanced around to her kin, seeing every one still sleeping. Sickness creeped up into her stomach. With quiet scurry, Evelyn hurried out the indirect access. Over the patio railing and onto the withering grass was the place where the substance of her stomach discharged. She spit the excess bile from her mouth. Weariness started to overpower her body similarly as.

"Everything okay?"

The unexpected voice made Evelyn bounce. She went to its source and felt better knowing it's anything but a dead individual.

"I'm fine. Required some natural air." Evelyn didn't anticipate that Daniel should be over here. She must've woken him when she got up from the love seat.

"Horse crap." Daniel moved to remain close to her, offering her some food. She took it thankfully, expecting to get the acidic taste from her mouth.

"Bad dream." It was everything she could say. Daniel definitely knew what was going on with it. No compelling reason to make a plunge further. "Please accept my apologies assuming I woke you up."

He shook his head. "You didn't."

"Bologna."

They took a gander at one another briefly. In this short delay the two of them came to the quiet agreement that they have met their match in one another. No falsehoods. No casual banter. No horse crap.

"For what reason did you get around here?" Evelyn didn't meet his eyes when posing this inquiry, rather she carefully concentrated on the states of the timberline something like thirty feet opposite them.

Daniel didn't answer right away. He considered the inquiry. Clearly he would need to come clean with her, however it would sound unusual coming from him. A piece of him needed to make up some untruth, yet Evelyn would see straight through it. She generally does.

"I'm stressed over you." He was unable to check out her all things considered.

"You don't need to be."

"That doesn't change the way that I am."

Quietness filled the virus air that whipped against their uncovered skin. It desensitized their ears in an enjoyably diverting manner. Evelyn didn't have any idea how to react. This is perhaps the longest discussion they've had. An hour passed during this time of quiet. It comprised of tranquility and off-kilter investigates the woods outline.

"Come on." Daniel drove away from the railing. "How about we return to rest."

Similarly as Daniel dismissed, Evelyn took hold of his hand. He froze.

"Much obliged to you. Truly."

He just gestured.

•••

Promptly the following morning, Sebastian slashed logs for fire while Evelyn gathered it. The gloves on her hands kept the splinters under control. She stacked them in the carport to dry.

Blair and the remainder of the gathering, barring Graham, cooperated to develop a greater amount of the expansion. Daniel adhered to Blair's guidance at each turn, inquisitive to learn en route. Sporadically he would glance out a window towards where Sebastian slashed wood. He wouldn't concede to himself that the explanation for his periodic looks have something to manage the lady helping convey the logs. Rather, he will persuade himself he's simply determining the status of them on the grounds that... indeed, in light of the fact that he can. As a head of the gathering, Daniel can do however he sees fit. This thinking is sufficient for him.

This is chiefly what the day comprises of. Dividing logs and working onto the expansion.
At the point when she would be in the carport, she can hear the beating of mallet to nail and the scratching of boots across the floor. At the point when she ends up outside, her look floats to the windows. Especially the window exhibiting Daniel. His sleeves are pushed back to his elbows, uncovering his intricate tattoo and etched lower arms. As he raises his arms to pound in another nail his shirt lifts up somewhat. Evelyn turns away, criticizing herself for the chance of getting found out.

"Something at the forefront of your thoughts?" Sebastian took a respite in his swinging, extending the muscles in his arms.

"No." It could never have happened to her that Sebastian could be the one to get her.

"You sure?" A little, insidious grin plays all the rage. "Has nothing to do with, perhaps, Daniel?"

Assuming anybody's glare is a thing to be dreaded, it ought to be Evelyn's. Be that as it may, it had no grasp on Sebastian. He can own directly to her middle.

"He is alluring, yet he's a dick." Sebastian dodged as Evelyn sent her gloves rushing towards his head. "Recently I've seen he's been to a lesser degree a dick to you and as yet unchanged poop chute to most of us."

How should Evelyn react? Daniel has still been his typical self regardless of their new and exceptionally concise discussions. With those to the side he is still Daniel.

"No, he's-"

Sebastian put his hatchet down in peril. "Everyone except you can see it."

"Please accept my apologies, everyone?" Evelyn doesn't comprehend. Is this some subject of discussion now? "Who's all discussing this?"

"It's not talking. It's more similar to a look that somebody imparts to another person who has a similar idea."

Evelyn topped off the wheel barrel with the remainder of the logs and took them up to the carport, totally disregarding Sebastian's gets back to come. She stacked the logs against the divider until she could never again arrive at the top. Just a modest bunch stay at the lowest possible quality.

As Evelyn stressed to put the following log on the heap, a hand delicately took it from her grip and put it where she couldn't reach.

"You realize I'm just playing with you." Sebastian stacked the other logs.

"I do." Evelyn moaned, brushing hair out of her face. "You're worrying me."

"I don't intend to do that." He remained by her, his hand on her shoulder. Sebastian knows about what she went through. Perhaps irritating her with regards to Daniel isn't awesome right now. Sometime in the future, maybe.

"I know."

Sebastian kissed her brow and afterward pushed her towards the entryway. "Get inside. Eat something. I'll see you later."

Evelyn grinned. It developed almost to her ears. "Bye, Sebastian."

•••

"...then there's the issue of permanency." Graham went over his rundowns and charts with Evelyn as he lay laid up until his condition improves. He examined possible choices for the gathering. An extended nursery is one of many. Perhaps a little homestead with any animals they may go over. Maybe extra lodging units around the property.

"I've provided you with a guide of the property." Evelyn feels great realizing Graham feels valuable. "Show me what we should work here and I will get it going."

Graham sat upstanding against a pile of cushions, outlining endlessly. Marcy moved to one side and momentarily talked with Evelyn away from Graham's ears.

"Much thanks to you, once more, for getting his medication. We are appreciative to you." Marcy embraced her chief firmly.

"There's no compelling reason to say thanks to me. You're every one of my kin. Your requirements are my necessities. Remember that." With this said Evelyn passed on Marcy and Graham to their protection.

For the remainder of the day Evelyn stayed in the workplace. She concentrated on various archives relating to the property and the house. She found where the septic tank is, and even went out into the yard to ensure its careful area. A touch of natural air significantly helped her lungs.

"Eve, do you have a second?" Autumn moved toward Evelyn from behind.

"Sure. What's happening?"

Pre-winter glanced back at the carport and afterward to Evelyn once more. "Daniel needs to converse with you at whatever point you have the opportunity. He said he needs to show something to you."

Evelyn's stomach couldn't resist the opportunity to persuade her that Daniel discovered her gazing at him. "Where could he be?"

"In the expansion."

Evelyn felt like she was doing the stroll to her demise. Her stomach rolled steadily. Imagine a scenario where she simply gets a move on and runs back to the house. Stowing away in a storeroom for an hour shouldn't be excessively risky. No. Everything's all good. She will confront him with certainty. Notwithstanding, when the acknowledgment hit that they are the main two in the expansion, that very certainty flew out the window.

Daniel went to meet Evelyn's reluctant look. "Simply the individual I was searching for."

"I was told you needed to converse with me."

"How about we take a walk." He gestured his head towards the brook.

Evelyn's heart dropped into her stomach. He needed to have seen her concise looks at him. It's the main clarification. For what other reason would Daniel recommend that he and Evelyn go for a stroll to an obscure area, though on the property, yet an area with essentially more security than elsewhere inside a structure.

On the stroll there, no discussion is had. Nervousness deteriorates in Evelyn and she can't determine what feelings Daniel is feeling. He seems like a clean canvas. Inert. Plain. Indeed, not plain.

"Did I accomplish something wrong?" She can't take the quiet any longer.

With most extreme perplexity, Daniel's face turns. Did she truly ask him that? "No."

This single word reaction is the main sort of reaction she got. Daniel strolled down the side of the bank, offering his hand to Evelyn for balance. She took it. The inconsistent messages were driving her up a divider. Maybe she's seeing them wrong, or she's adding a lot to them.

On the slight segment of stone shore they sit. The briskness of the stones douses into their pants. If not for the sun to keep them warm, they would be a shuddering wreck.

"What's happening?" Evelyn folded her arms over her knees.

"You know when we saw that person in the drug store?"

"Yeah..."

Now in the discussion Daniel started to tinker with one of the stones at his feet.

"Assuming it would help your lamenting interaction, and help you to have an improved outlook, I could cover him for you. However, provided that you need."

Quickly, the restless inclination in Evelyn's stomach dispersed. It doesn't has anything to do with her incidental glances toward him. What occurred to her not long after is the way that Daniel needs to return to the drug store where they experienced the dead body. A virus surge of dread overpowered her detects. Evelyn would rather not return. She believes she ought to stay away from and smother until further notice.

"You seem as though you're pondering something."

Evelyn couldn't talk. Her entire being was pooled towards keeping her tears under control. Tragically, she was unable to control the redness in her eyes nor the snugness in her throat.

"I, um..." She constrained out an excruciating breath. "Some portion of me never needs to return."

There are a few things people aren't intended to see. Particularly when it's the body of somebody you've known for what seems like forever.

"We don't need to."

Evelyn shook her head, attempting to sort out her clashing sentiments. "My stomach is letting me know I need to."

Daniel took this second to really check out her. He could detect her inward fight. Various feelings played all over. Evelyn's eyes show everything. The dread. The affection. The pity. Everything.

"Then, at that point, we will." He gradually arrived at his hand towards her, putting it on top of her own. One delicate crush was all it took for the conduits to deliver. She was unable to keep down her trouble any longer. It overpowered her detects.

"I knew him." She cried into her hands. "He was my chief. I've known him since before I could walk."

All while Evelyn uncovered little subtleties of her past, Daniel delicately ran his thumb over her knuckles. Now and again, she would wipe away her tears with a sleeve. In some cases she would squeeze the extension of her nose, regardless of whether in torment or be it an interruption Daniel could never know. After some time she quieted down. Her breathing got back to business as usual and her tears dried.

"When will we go cover him?"

Daniel could see the sadness and agony in her eyes, the apprehension about seeing the inert body of a man she once knew. In any case, assurance and love eclipsed these sentiments.

"At the point when you're prepared."

THE END

www.ingramcontent.com/pod-product-compliance
Lightning Source LLC
LaVergne TN
LVHW050349160826
845677LV00014B/3871